This book belongs to

_____

_____

_____

At the BOARDWALK

For Sara and Maggie

—K.R.F.

For my family

—M.A.

tiger tales
an imprint of ME Media, LLC
5 River Road, Suite 128, Wilton, CT 06897
Published in the United States 2012
Text copyright © 2012 Kelly Ramsdell Fineman
Illustrations copyright © 2012 Mónica Armiño
CIP data is available
(Hardcover) ISBN-13: 978-1-58925-104-5
(Hardcover) ISBN-10: 1-58925-104-0
(Paperback) ISBN-13: 978-1-58925-431-2
(Paperback) ISBN-10: 1-58925-431-7
Printed in China
LPP 0611
For more insight and activities,
visit us at www.tigertalesbooks.com

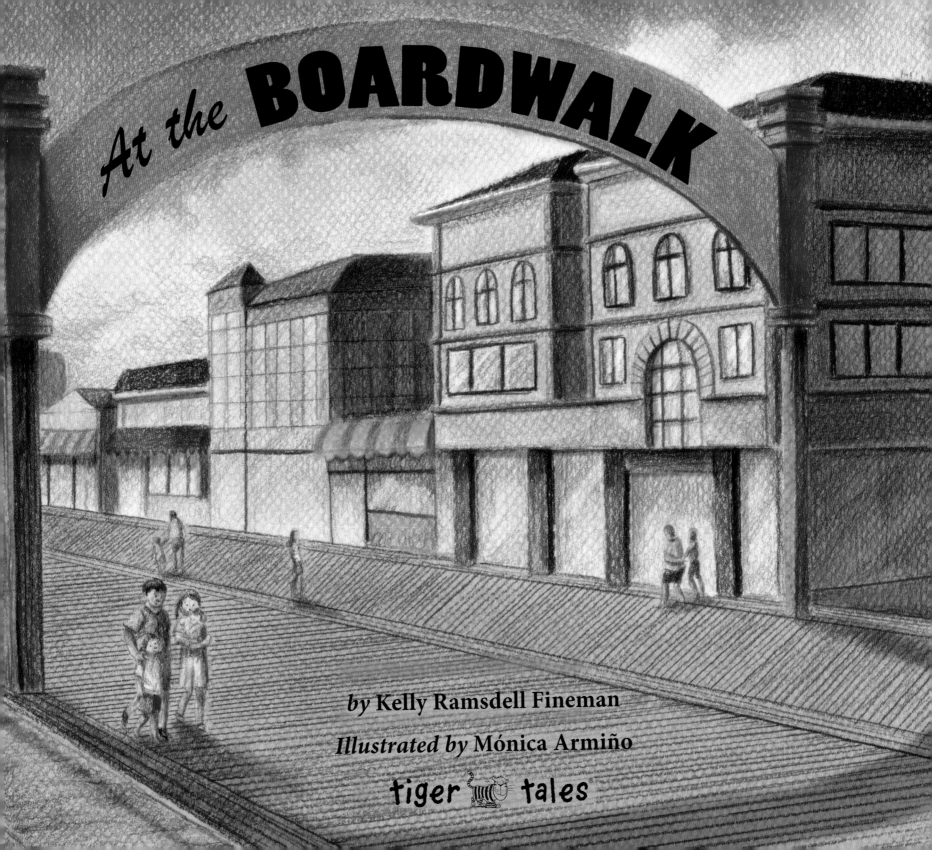

At the BOARDWALK

by Kelly Ramsdell Fineman

Illustrated by Mónica Armiño

tiger tales

At the boardwalk
by the sea
Days are spent with family

Life relaxes; time is free

At the boardwalk

by the sea

At the boardwalk
    in the fog
Grab the stroller, bring the dog
Families take a morning jog

At the boardwalk
in the fog

At the boardwalk
    bubbles fly
Bumping into passersby
Salt-air breezes, kites up high
At the boardwalk
    bubbles fly

At the boardwalk

in the sun

Take a break from beach-time fun

Ice cream cones for everyone!

At the boardwalk

in the sun

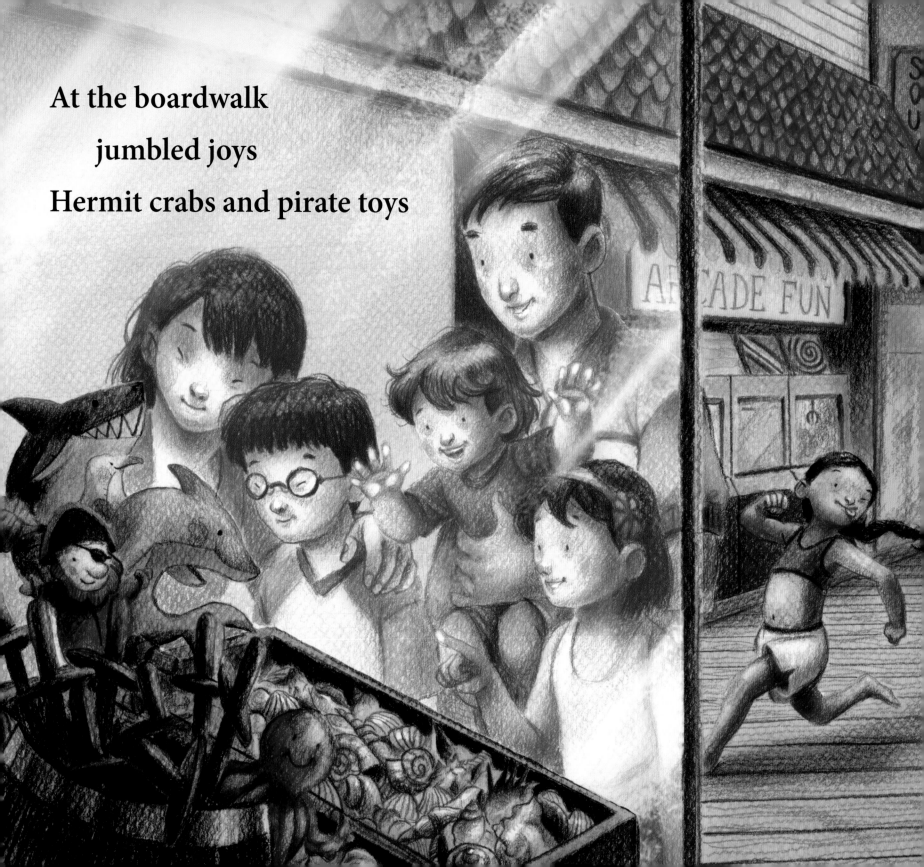

At the boardwalk
    jumbled joys
Hermit crabs and pirate toys

Arcade games make lots of noise

At the boardwalk

jumbled joys

At the boardwalk
when it rains
Grumpy gulls are weather vanes

Everyone around complains

At the boardwalk

when it rains

At the boardwalk
day or night
Treats for every appetite

Popcorn – taffy – fudge, delight
At the boardwalk
day or night

At the boardwalk

near the sand

Sunset paints the sky and land

Shadows lengthen; stars expand
At the boardwalk

near the sand

At the boardwalk

one last ride

Oompah music, sit astride

Carouseling, side by side

At the boardwalk

one last ride

At the boardwalk
on the pier
Music plays for all to hear

People hold their loved ones near
At the boardwalk
on the pier

At the boardwalk
day is done
Sleepy after evening fun

Strolling home – no need to run

At the boardwalk

day is done

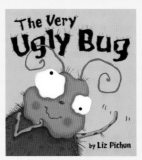

The Very Ugly Bug
by Liz Pichon
ISBN-13: 978-1-58925-404-6
ISBN-10: 1-58925-404-X

Itsy Bitsy Spider
by Keith Chapman
Illustrated by Jack Tickle
ISBN-13: 978-1-58925-407-7
ISBN-10: 1-58925-407-4

The 108th Sheep
by Ayano Imai
ISBN-13: 978-1-58925-420-6
ISBN-10: 1-58925-420-1

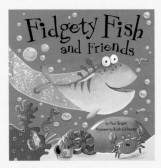

Fidgety Fish and Friends
by Paul Bright
Illustrated by Ruth Galloway
ISBN-13: 978-1-58925-409-1
ISBN-10: 1-58925-409-0

Explore the world of tiger tales!

More fun-filled and exciting stories await you!
Look for these titles and more at your local library or bookstore.
And have fun reading!

tiger tales

5 River Road, Suite 128, Wilton, CT 06897

Good Night, Sleep Tight!
by Claire Freedman
Illustrated by Rory Tyger
ISBN-13: 978-1-58925-405-3
ISBN-10: 1-58925-405-8

Boris and the Snoozebox
by Leigh Hodgkinson
ISBN-13: 978-1-58925-421-3
ISBN-10: 1-58925-421-X

A Very Special Hug
by Steve Smallman
Illustrated by Tim Warnes
ISBN-13: 978-1-58925-410-7
ISBN-10: 1-58925-410-4

Just for You!
by Christine Leeson
Illustrated by Andy Ellis
ISBN-13: 978-1-58925-408-4
ISBN-10: 1-58925-408-2